JUST ME AND MY MOM

BY
MERCER MAYER

For my new son Benjamin
and his Momma

A GOLDEN BOOK • NEW YORK

Golden Books Publishing Company, Inc., Racine, Wisconsin 53404

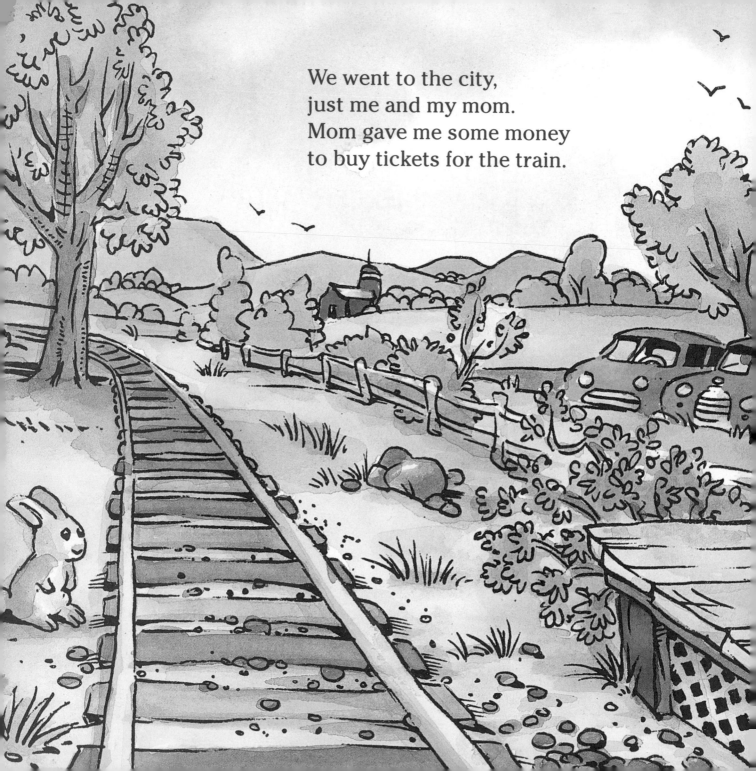

We went to the city,
just me and my mom.
Mom gave me some money
to buy tickets for the train.

TICKETS

I wanted to help Mom get on the train
but the steps were too high.
So Mom helped me instead.

But when the conductor came by,
the tickets were gone.
So Mom paid the conductor
some more money.

The city was very busy.
I held Mom's hand so she
wouldn't be scared.

We went to the Museum
of Natural History.
They had rooms full of
old dinosaur bones.

I picked up a little dinosaur egg
to show to my mom.
But someone ran up and grabbed it.
I wasn't going to hurt it.

I tried on some costumes,
just for Mom.
But the museum guard
didn't like that.

Then we went next door
to the Aquarium.

There were lots of fish
in a big tank of water.

They had some seals doing a show.
Mom got mad because
she couldn't find me.
I ran up front to get
a closer look at the seals.

We went to the art museum,
but it only had a lot of weird pictures
and I was getting tired.

After that, we went to a very
nice restaurant for lunch.
We didn't stay, though.

We decided to have a hot dog from
a stand. That was more fun anyway.

Mom wanted to go to a big store
full of dresses and stuff like that. Yuck.

Mom even made me try on some clothes.
She bought me a new suit.
Some guy measured me and stuck pins all over
my clothes.

We passed by the toys.
I found the stuffed animal
I always wanted
but Mom said, "It's time to go."

We took a taxi to the train station.
I got to ride in the front seat.
The taxi driver drove real fast.
That was cool.

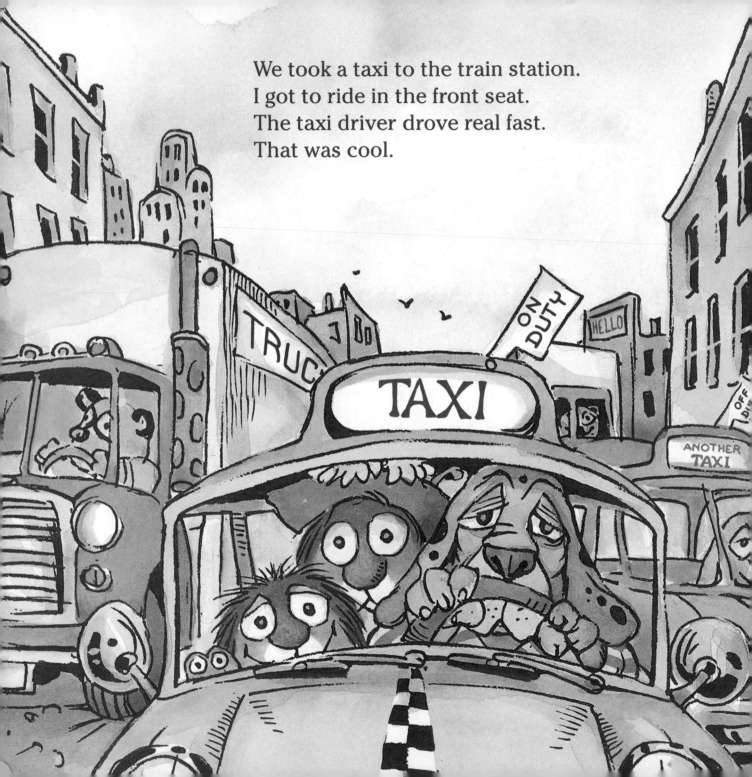

I let Mom buy the tickets this time. She said she didn't have enough money to buy more tickets if these got lost.
"Good idea, Mom!"

We had fun, just me and my mom.
I even stayed awake
all the way home — well, almost.